17 CAMPFIRE STORIES FOR FAMILIES AND KIDS

A SCARY AND FUN STORY AND TALES COLLECTION
TO TELL AROUND THE CAMPFIRE

ELVIN CREATIONS

© **Copyright EDVIN SZOLCSAK 2021 - All rights reserved.**

The content contained within this book may not be reproduced, duplicated or transmitted without direct written permission from the author or the publisher.

Under no circumstances will any blame or legal responsibility be held against the publisher, or author, for any damages, reparation, or monetary loss due to the information contained within this book. Either directly or indirectly. You are responsible for your own choices, actions, and results.

Legal Notice:

This book is copyright protected. This book is only for personal use. You cannot amend, distribute, sell, use, quote or paraphrase any part, or the content within this book, without the consent of the author or publisher.

Disclaimer Notice:

Please note the information contained within this document is for educational and entertainment purposes only. All effort has been executed to present accurate, up to date, and reliable, complete information. No warranties of any kind are declared or implied. Readers acknowledge that the author is not engaging in the rendering of legal, financial, medical or professional advice. The content within this book has been derived from various sources. Please consult a licensed professional before attempting any techniques outlined in this book.

By reading this document, the reader agrees that under no circumstances is the author responsible for any losses, direct or indirect, which are incurred as a result of the use of the information contained within this document, including, but not limited to, — errors, omissions, or inaccuracies.

CONTENTS

Who Are We?   5

1. Hollow Of The Axe Murder   7
2. Open Wireless Network Connection   10
3. The Story Of Bear & Squirrel   13
4. Tale Of Vinder Viper   17
5. The Bloody Finger's Spirit   20
6. Maniac Or Mouse   23
7. The Ghost With One Yellow Eye Is A Ghost With One Black Eye   26
8. The Woman Who Was Staring   29
9. Partner In The Room   31
10. One More Space   34
11. Terror Tombspace   36
12. A Serious Problem   38
13. The Casket   40
14. To The Bone   43
15. The Lady Of The Smart Ring   46
16. The Scroll Of Piggy   49
17. Underneath The Bed Is A Killer   52

We would like to give a big thanks to our supporters who read the book! If you enjoy the book please leave a review or rating on amazon!

If you want to get access or news about our new books or be part of a great community, please

Scan the QR Code below and like our page on facebook!

WHO ARE WE?

Elvin Creations, in particular, deals in the creation of Children's books. We are a group of friends, parents and authors. This was our dream and we're finally on the verge of achieving it. This book serves the purpose of bringing parents and kids close to each other so that they can do more interesting and interactive activities together. It's an amalgamation of seventeen short campfire stories to tell in the dark and out in the forest with your friends, family, or parents. It is loaded with funny and spooky stories that both parents and children can enjoy.

At the moment, we're working on creating our content on social media sites such as Facebook and Instagram. They'll provide us platforms to communicate with people, giving us an opportunity to improve ourselves. Also, we'll be providing a website for the business soon. This'll give us a better chance to enhance our brand's marketing. In the near future, we'd love to create more and more coloring and activity books.

We do hope that you'll enjoy our short stories and that they bring some fun to your family, and create more special moments between kids and parents.

1

HOLLOW OF THE AXE MURDER

Susan and Ned were travelling along a wooded stretch of freeway that was devoid of traffic. The dark sky lit up as lightning flashed and thunder roared in the torrential downpour.

Susan said, "I think we should call it a day."

With a nod of his head, Ned expressed his agreement. The vehicle began to slide on the wet pavement when he applied the brakes. They skidded off the road and came to a halt at the bottom of a steep incline.

Ned suddenly turned around, pale and shaking, to see if Susan was okay. After she nodded, Ned relaxed and gazed out the rain-soaked windows.

He told her, "I'm going to see how bad it is," and stepped out into the squall. He walked around the front of the car, his figure blurry in the headlights. Drenched, he hopped in beside her a few moments later. "The car isn't badly damaged," he explained, "but we're wheel-deep in mud. I'll have to go for assistance."

Susan inhaled deeply before nervously swallowing. In this case, there would be no swift rescue. Ned instructed her to switch off the lights and lock the doors until he returned.

Hollow of the Axe Murder. Even though he hadn't said the name aloud, they both knew, when he ordered her to lock the car, Ned was contemplating something. A guy took an axe to his wife and stabbed her to death in a furious rage over a supposed affair. The husband's axe-wielding spirit was said to haunt this stretch of road.

Susan heard a shriek, a loud thump, and a peculiar gurgling noise outside the car. But in the dark night, she couldn't see anything.

She slid down in her seat, terrified. She sat in silence for a few seconds before hearing something else. Bump. Bump. Bump. It was a gentle sound, as if blown by the wind.

A bright light suddenly shone into the car. An official-sounding voice told her to exit the car. Ned must've met a cop. After unlocking the door, Susan took a step out of the car. When her eyes adjusted to the bright light, she noticed it.

Ned's body was hanging by his feet from a tree near the car. He was almost decapitated because his throat had been cut so deeply. His body thumped against the tree as the wind swung it back and forth.

Susan screamed and dashed away from the voice and towards the light. As she got closer to it, she realized the light wasn't coming from a flashlight. A glowing figure of a man stood there, smiling and wielding a huge, powerful, and unmistakable axe. She took a few steps back from the glowing figure before she ran into the car.

"Playing around when my back was turned?" the ghost murmured, caressing the sharp blade of the axe with his fingertips. "You've been particularly mischievous."

The gleam of the axe blade in the eerie, incandescent light was the last thing she saw.

2

OPEN WIRELESS NETWORK CONNECTION

When I told them there was an open wireless network in range, aptly named "Free Wifi," they didn't believe me. It was slow, but that wasn't the problem. We were camping in the middle of nowhere (Tar Hollow Woods, for any Ohioans out there.) We parked the truck about a mile down the trail, and it was a fifteen-minute drive from there to the only freeway ramp. We were, to put it mildly, a long way from civilization.

After we finished checking in on Facebook and responding to snapchats, my friends and I played a game of locating the source of the signal. Mike and I took one route, while Marco and Sean took the other. In three minutes, we were all back at the construction site. After 185 paces in my direction and 250 paces in the opposite direction, the signal disappeared.

In order to triangulate the source's location, we decided to go in a third direction, as Sean suggested. Marco kept track of the steps, Mike watched the signal indicator, and Sean and I looked for something that resembled a router.

Mike told Marco to stop counting about a hundred feet in. The signal was at maximum power. I looked for anything that lit up, whether it was flashing LEDs, running wires, or anything else. Marco speculated that it could be a forgotten pocket wifi hotspot from another camper (though that was unlikely, since there was no 3G coverage out there.) However, we came up empty-handed.

We called it quits on our search and returned to the campground. At that point, the wifi signal disappeared. The sun was setting and a thick fog was forming. Despite our fears, we agreed to pack our belongings and return to the truck on foot. We found that we'd been robbed. Our tents had been knocked over, our bags were torn open, and our food had vanished.

The fact that the thieves left our laptops and cameras behind struck me as odd right away. After a closer inspection, they simply took the food and drinks. That was, in my opinion, the most terrifying part. We stuffed everything we could into our ripped up bags and dashed for the truck. Mike didn't say anything about checking our phones until we were in the truck. The wifi signal had fully recovered its strength. Shivers ran down my spine when I saw the connection's name: RUN, BOYS, RUN.

3

THE STORY OF BEAR & SQUIRREL

Bear was out walking around a long time ago, before animals had lost the ability to communicate. As he walked, Bear boasted.

"Hmmph!" he cried.

"I am the most powerful of all the animals. Hmmph! I am the largest of all the animals. Hmmph! I can do anything because I am Bear. If I want people to do my bidding, I just have to tell them I'm Bear. Anything is possible for me."

Just as Bear said that, a small voice from the ground spoke up. It stated, "You can't do everything."

Bear drew his brows together and lowered his head. Squirrel poked his head above the surface of his burrow.

Bear looked down at him and said, "I, Bear, can do anything I want."

"If this is true, can you tell the sun not to rise in the morning?" Squirrel asked curiously.

"Yes," Bear said after a brief pause.

"That's something I'm capable of. I have the ability to stop the sun from rising. The sun will not rise tomorrow, in fact."

"That's good," Squirrel said. "I'm going to stay and watch." And the two of them sat down right away.

As the sun began to set, Bear and Squirrel turned east, hoping that the sun would not rise the next morning. As they sat there all night, Bear prayed under his breath.

He said, "The sun won't rise. The sun will not rise today. It's under my command. The sun isn't going to come up today."

Squirrel, on the other hand, was muttering under his breath, "The sun is going to rise.

The sun will soon rise. Bear is going to look like a fool. It is going to be a lovely day."

A sliver of light shone in the east as the night came to a close. Bear started chanting louder, "The sun will not rise. The sun isn't going to come up today."

The little Squirrel next to him said, "The sun is going to rise. The sun will soon rise."

As the sun rose above the horizon, Bear chanted as loudly as he could, facing the rising sun and pleading with it not to come up. The sun broke through the horizon, signalling the start of a new day. Squirrel began to laugh. He rolled over and over, amusement on his face.

"Bear is a fool!" he cried. "Bear is such a knucklehead! The sun is shining brightly, the sun is shining brightly, the sun is shining brightly! The sun has risen!"

Whomp. Whomp. Whomp. Whomp. A big paw trampled on Squirrel.

"Indeed, the sun did come up," Bear said as he held Squirrel on the ground. "However, you will never see another sunrise!"

Squirrel realised he'd made a blunder. He paused for a moment, thinking. He said, "Oh Bear, you're right to kill me. I'm just a clumsy little Squirrel who doesn't know what he's doing. In the eyes of the world, I am unworthy and insignificant. Bear, you're the best of them all, and if you could just lift your paw a little so I could catch my breath, I'd tell you how lovely you are before you kill me."

Bear said, "That's a great idea."

As Bear lifted his paw a little, Squirrel scooted out and dashed as quickly as he could for his hole. Whoosh! Bear whipped his big paw out! His claws scraped Squirrel's back as he dove into his hole.

Squirrel spent the entire winter in his hole, recovering from his back wounds. When he first came out in the spring, he had stripes on his back as well. Squirrel's stripes are still visible today, and they may serve as a reminder to you, as they do Squirrel, to be careful who you mock. You could end up being the stupid one in the end. That's how the story of Squirrel and his pals started.

4

TALE OF VINDER VIPER

A man inherited a home from his great uncle, who died in the war many years ago. The mansion, located on a hill outside of a village in the next state, was said to be haunted. The man travelled to town to inspect the house, which he discovered to be a beautiful, but extremely old mansion in excellent condition. As a result, he made the decision to settle down and enjoy his inheritance.

Late one night, a few weeks after he moved in, the phone rang. When he picked it up, a voice said, "My name is Vinder Viper. I'll be there in two weeks!"

The phone rang again and the caller immediately hung up before the man could say anything. He was completely shaken by this. The next day, he looked up "Vinder Viper" under the heading of "snakes" on the internet, but came up empty-handed.

The phone rang late one night after a week of no worries.

"My name is Vinder Viper. I'll be there in a week!"

The man hung up because he had no idea what a Vinder Viper was. This made him uneasy. No one had ever heard of such a viper, and he had inquired around town without result.

The phone rang four days later late at night. "My name is Vinder Viper. I'll be there in two days!" The man became more and more concerned.

The phone rang the next night.

"My name is Vinder Viper. Tomorrow, I'll be there!"

The man was obviously horrified by now.

The phone rang the next evening.

"Vinder Viper is my name. In one hour I'll be there!" The man attempted to leave, but his vehicle's battery died.

The phone rang nearly an hour later.

"Vinder Viper is my name. In two minutes, I'll be there!"

The man rushed around the house, locking all of the windows and doors before dialling

911. The cops were on their way to the scene.

Soon after, there was a knock at the door.

"Is that the police?" the man asked as he pushed open the door a crack.

"No, I'm the finder's viper, and every month I visit to Vash your windows."

THE BLOODY FINGER'S SPIRIT

There was an old abandoned home in a small village not far from here. No one walked near it because it was rumoured to be haunted.

One day, a group of locals sat in a coffee shop discussing courage. One man, in particular, was boasting loudly.

"I'm not afraid of anything!"

"Oh yeah?" his companion inquired. "I'm sure you wouldn't want to spend the night in that abandoned house by yourself!"

Because he didn't want to admit he was afraid, he agreed to spend the night in the house.

At dusk, he arrived at the house by himself. He went through each room and found nothing unusual. He went upstairs, spread his sleeping bag on the floor and tried to sleep.

He'd just dozed off when he heard a faint noise downstairs. Moving his head, he attempted to decipher what it was. He thought he heard someone muttering, "I'm the bloody finger's phantom! I've arrived in the lobby!"

The man convinced himself that he was dreaming. He figured it was just the wind.

"I am the ghost of the bloody finger!" he heard again, a little louder this time. "I have arrived at the bottom of the stairwell!"

The man exclaimed, "My imagination is going crazy! I'm just going to bed, and it'll be morning before I know it."

But then, even louder, he heard, "I'm the bloody finger's phantom! I've gotten to the top of the stairwell!"

The man crawled into his sleeping bag but the ghost was still approaching.

"I'm the bloody finger's phantom! I'm in the second-floor corridor!"

The man hid his head beneath his pillow, but the ghost got closer.

"I'm the bloody finger's phantom! I'm on my way to your room!"

Fear gripped the man's body. The door swung open with a squeaky sound.

"I'm the bloody finger's phantom! I'm in your room!" the speaker exclaimed.

In the doorway, the ghost stopped.

"I am the bloody finger's ghost!" the phantom yelled, then paused. "Do you have a bandaid?"

MANIAC OR MOUSE

At the end of the street, there was once a deserted cottage near the forest's edge. My brother and I used to go to hang out and play, despite — or perhaps because of — our mother's wishes for us to stay away.

We walked over there one warm summer evening, flashlights in hand. Despite how creepy it was, we egged each other on and, as usual, crawled in through the kitchen window. We'd brought a deck of cards with us and played poker at the kitchen table when a scraping noise came from upstairs.

My brother said, "It's probably just a mouse."

It seemed plausible since the house had been empty for years.

We listened to one more scraping sound a minute later, this time coming from the opposite side of the building's stairwell. My brother and I exchanged a few fearful glances before laughing nervously. Because we didn't want to show that we were afraid, we dealt a new hand of cards and continued playing.

Then, just outside the kitchen door, there was a clank of metal against metal. We couldn't see anything in the dim hallway light, but something had made contact with the old metal fireplace guard, and we knew it.

"OK, that's not a mouse," I said.

"Let's get out of here!" we exclaimed.

My brother and I leapt to our feet and dashed towards the nearest window. I was the first to arrive and jumped out of it. He jumped out with both feet first and made a whooshing sound a fraction of a second later.

Mom was wringing her hands on the porch and we ran like our pants were on fire the entire way home.

She said, "Thank goodness you're home. There's a psychopath on the loose. According to the news, he escaped earlier today, and he's armed with a big butcher knife. They also said that he's on the lookout for young boys to kill. We should go inside. It's time for bed anyway."

Before following mom inside, my brother and I exchanged glances, still panting from the frantic rush.

As we made our way to the bedroom, she inquired, "Hey, what happened to your shirt?

Did it get snagged on something? Wow, this is a ripper. What's the reason for this?"

She pointed to a long gash in the back of my brother's shirt, which stretched almost to his waist.

When he jumped out the window, what caused the whooshing sound? All we know is that the maniac was arrested a week later after slicing open five young boys in town, all in abandoned houses similar to the one we'd been in.

7

THE GHOST WITH ONE YELLOW EYE IS A GHOST WITH ONE BLACK EYE

A tavern stood on the road leading from the countryside to the city in the early 1900s. It was a popular break point for travellers to eat and rest. Except for one haunted room, the entire pub would be packed.

A fight at the tavern years ago resulted in a man losing his eye. The others at the tavern took him to that room when he passed out. He didn't make it out of there and died. Since then, that room seemed to be haunted by his ghost.

The tavern received a visit from a cowboy one day. The old proprietor informed him that only the haunted room was available.

"I wrestle with bulls and rope them every day," the cowboy explained. "I don't mind ghosts," he declared as he entered the room.

While taking a bath later that night, the cowboy overheard a booming voice say, "I am the ghost with one black eye."

The cowboy became frantic and looked around for help, but there was none to be found. He wrapped himself in his towel and bolted.

A barmaid requested a room on another occasion, but the tavern was completely full.

Only one room was left, according to the old man, and it was haunted.

"I've seen the most violent of men where I work," the barmaid said. "I'm not afraid of ghosts. I'll take the room."

Just like the cowboy, she heard those same words in the booming voice as she tucked herself into bed that night. She felt a shiver run down her spine. She dressed, grabbed her belongings, and dashed out of the tavern.

A couple with a son arrived a few days later. The couple desired their own room, but the only other option for their son was the haunted room.

"Cool, a real ghost," the son exclaimed. "I'm going to live there!"

When the boy turned off the lights to go to bed that night, he heard a voice say, "I am the ghost with one black eye."

"Well, I am a boy scout," the young boy said calmly as he turned on the bed lamp. "You will become a ghost with two black eyes if you don't keep your mouth shut from now on."

The silence was deafening. The boy went to sleep quietly after turning off the light. The ghost hasn't bothered or scared anyone since that day.

8

THE WOMAN WHO WAS STARING

To return home from work, a woman named Sharon boarded a late-night train. She found three people seated on the opposite berth as she sat down on the train. A woman wearing a hoodie stood between two scrawny-looking men. She was leaning against the compartment's wall, her head resting gently on it. While the trio as a whole was unremarkable, Sharon noted that the woman in the hoodie was staring at her incessantly. She didn't even bother to blink. Sharon grinned at her, but the other woman didn't return the grin. It made

Sharon feel uneasy, so she grabbed a book from her bag and held it up to her face, covering it.

The train came to a halt at a station. A man stood beside Sharon on the train.

"These three aren't what they seem," the man said as the train continued on its journey. "At the next station, get off with me. Believe me when I say this - don't worry; there are plenty of cops there, so you'll be safe."

Sharon was surprised and didn't respond. She set the book down and turned to face the lady in the hoodie. Her gaze was fixed on her! The stare was terrifying, and she was itching to get off at the next station.

At the following station, the man and Sharon descended. A sigh of relief escaped his

lips.

"Thank God!" he exclaimed. "I'm a physician. The lady you saw on the train was taken to the hospital and later pronounced dead. Her body went missing a few hours later."

PARTNER IN THE ROOM

Charlotte and her friends from school had gone camping. The campsite was located in the middle of the woodland. Charlotte's teacher informed her that she would be sharing her room with Emily, who was a happy, cheerful young lady. Emily had a hair band that Charlotte really liked. It was a small band with a pinkish star on one of the edges.

Charlotte and Emily grew closer as a result of their shared experiences. They shared a bunk bed with Emily sleeping on the bottom and Charlotte sleeping on the top.

Emily invited Charlotte to join her for a meal one day.

"Emily, what is it?"

"Charlotte, I need to talk to you about something. Our bed makes me feel uneasy. At midnight, I keep feeling someone tap from underneath. I'm afraid to look, so I don't."

"How do you know it's someone?" Charlotte asked. "Perhaps you're just dreaming."

Charlotte reassured Emily that the next time the tapping occurred, she would look under the bed. Charlotte went to bed after dinner a few days later. She found Emily, sitting on her bed, legs folded, and a wide grin on her face.

Charlotte, perplexed, asked, "Why're you smiling?"

"I believe I've found the source of the tapping from beneath the bed. I don't think there'll be any more commotion. Wait a minute while I brush my teeth. I'll be back to tell you the rest of the story."

Emily stood up and walked to the bathroom. Charlotte sat on the edge of the bed. She heard tapping from underneath in a matter of seconds, catching her off guard. She couldn't see how there would be any tapping at this point. Charlotte bravely stood up and slowly lifted the sheet that covered the bottom of the bed. What she saw totally surprised her. It was Emily!

Emily cried, "What are you doing, Charlotte? Come down here with me before she returns."

Charlotte couldn't believe what she was seeing. Emily had just entered the bathroom, and she had just seen her. If Emily was here, she needed to find out who was in the bathroom.

Charlotte made a hasty trip to the restroom.

"Don't do that, Charlotte! You don't know what she'll do. Please come back. Wait a minute!" Emily's protests were ineffective in stopping Charlotte.

Charlotte swung the door to the bathroom open. Inside, there was no one.

"No one is here, Emily," she said.

Charlotte received no response. From the bathroom door, she shifted her gaze to the bed. Emily was gone, even though the main entrance had been shut. What had happened to her?

Charlotte was terrified at this point. She shifted her gaze to the toilet, where she noticed Emily's hairband on the washbasin. She took it in her hands, turned to face the mirror, and received the biggest shock of her life. The mirror reflected neither Charlotte nor Emily's band.

The reflection of the blank wall behind Charlotte was all that the mirror revealed.

ONE MORE SPACE

A young lady on her way to town made a pit stop at an old manor house to stay with friends. The carriage sweep at the front door was visible from her room. She struggled to sleep because it was a bright, moonlit night. She heard the sound of horses' hooves on the gravel outside her bedroom door and the sound of wheels as the clock struck twelve. Standing up, she walked over to the window to see who might be passing by at that hour. A hearse drove up to the door in the brilliant moonlight. It didn't have a coffin in it, but it was jam-packed with people.

The coachman was perched high on the box, turning his head as he approached the window.

"There's room for one more," he said calmly.

She drew the curtain, dashed back to her bed, and draped the bedclothes over her head. The next morning, she wasn't sure if it was a dream or if she had actually gotten out of bed and saw the hearse. Still, she was happy to leave the old house behind her and go up to town.

She was in a big store with an elevator, which was a cutting-edge feature at the time.

Being on the top floor and needing to go down, she went to the elevator.

"There's room for one more," the elevator operator said as she approached.

It was the face of the hearse's coachman.

"No, thank you," the young lady replied. "I'll take the stairs."

When she turned away, the elevator doors slammed shut, followed by a terrifying rush of screaming and yelling that ended with a loud clatter and thud. The elevator had collapsed, killing everyone inside.

TERROR TOMBSPACE

They were ghost hunters, Alan and Matt. They'd go to old cemeteries and try to elicit a spirit from an old tombstone. They began by placing their recorder on a particularly large and ornate headstone. They were scared to shine their flashlights on the stone to see the name engraved there, not to mention, trespassing in the graveyard at night was illegal. To get around the cemetery's caretaker, they climbed over the fence in the back.

"We'd like to talk to whoever lies beneath this stone," Matt said aloud as he turned on the recorder.

All they heard was a scratching noise coming from behind the tombstone as a response.

"Please tell us your name," Alan said calmly.

The only response was a scratching noise.

"We only wish to speak with you," Matt explained. "Please come forward and demonstrate."

The air turned chilly, and a tall, dark shadow emerged from behind the tombstone. They were engulfed by the shadow. Alan and Matt had numerous spiritual experiences and were unfazed. Then they realised, too late, that the apparition was trying to harm them. The shadow swept down and dragged them into the ground beneath the tombstone, burying them.

The recorder was discovered on the ground near the tombstone by the cemetery's caretaker the next morning. When he turned it on, he got the following reaction after each question.

"I am here..." the speaker said. "No living person ever mentions my name…I will be the last person you ever see if I show myself…I have both of you!" the voice exclaimed.

The caretaker quietly picked up the recorder. He went to his tool shed and threw the recorder into a pile of several others, knowing that he had the only proof that anyone had been in the cemetery and by the tombstone.

12

A SERIOUS PROBLEM

Maddy and Sue, two young girls who spent a lot of time together, were best friends. They wanted to tell ghost stories while Sue stayed the night at Maddy's. Maddy told her older brother a story about stabbing a blade into a grave, and the individual buried there would reach out and grab you and pull you into the grave.

Sue was dubious about the story. Maddy agreed, but in spite of the fact that it was only a story, she was hesitant to try it.

"I'm not afraid!" exclaimed Sue. "I'd take a chance."

Sue's bluff was called when Maddy challenged her to go to the cemetery down the road and prove she wasn't scared.

The girls walked downstairs to the kitchen and found a flashlight and a knife. Sue was determined to show that the story was a hoax and that she wasn't afraid of it. Maddy asked her not to go, but she set off into the dark night anyway.

Maddy waited for her pal at the kitchen table. The clock struck fifteen, then twenty minutes. After thirty minutes, Maddy went to her parents' room, woke them up, and informed them what had happened. As her father took a torch and went to the graveyard, she sobbed in her mother's embrace.

He was pale and shaken when he returned. He told Maddy and her mother what he had discovered in a solemn tone. Sue was laying on a grave, her hair entirely white. After hearing Maddy's explanation for why Sue was in the cemetery, the police were called, and the death was found to be accidental. Sue's nightgown hem was pierced by the knife as she stabbed it into the grave. She died of fright after believing she had been grabbed by the person buried there.

THE CASKET

A young man was going home on a dark, deserted street, on a dark night like this. He felt like he was being pursued as he walked through the gates of a small graveyard. He was startled to hear a bump behind him. He quickened his pace because he didn't want to look back. Bump. Bump. Bump.

The thudding behind him grew louder and closer. He finally turned around because he couldn't stand it any longer. When he saw a coffin standing on end, bumping down the road from side to side – bump, bump, bump – he was terrified. He ran for his life, but the coffin continued to approach at a faster rate than he could run.

BUMP. BUMP. BUMP.

The coffin got closer as the man grew tired of running. Terrified, the man grabbed a large metal trash can and threw it at it. The coffin continued to approach, unaffected.

BUMP. BUMP. BUMP.

He'd made it to his final destination. As he ran through his yard, he found the axe against the side of the tower, next to the woodpile. He snatched it and hurled it at the coffin, but it deflected. The coffin followed the man up the steps to the porch, pounding on the closed and locked front door.

BUMP. BUMP. BUMP.

He ran upstairs, grabbed his shotgun from the wall, and opened fire as the coffin went through the doorway. Despite this, the now partly shattered object continued on its way to him.

BUMP. BUMP. BUMP

In despair, the guy dashed into the bathroom, shut the door, and backed up as far as he could. He knew the coffin would merely smash the door down. The guy, on the other hand, was not going down without a fight. He snatched up a flask of cough medicine and threw it at the coffin. When the bottle shattered, cough syrup splattered all over the coffin. The coffin eventually came to a halt.

14

TO THE BONE

According to my grandmother, Captain Kidd drove up the Jersey coast looking for the perfect spot to bury his stolen booty, knowing the law was on his tail. And he discovered it on

Sandy Hook, in a grove of gnarled, wind-swept pines. The Adventure Galley slipped silently into Sandy Hook Harbor one moonless dark night. A gang of scurvy buccaneers armed with cutlasses and guns had rowed boatload after boatload of broad chests into the shore in front of two unseen watchers.

Their commander was Captain Kidd, a tall, confident man with red-whiskers and a cocked hat, who was immediately recognized by onlookers. The captain dragged his men away from the beach and into the pines. According to those who watched, the pirates were gone for a long time, long enough to bury any amount of treasure. They set sail early in the morning, rowed back to the Adventure Galley, and went into the fading light.

Of course, the onlookers kept their suspicions to themselves and scurried down to the pine grove with lanterns and shovels a few days later. But they didn't find a single gold coin, so they told their story to other good people in the area in frustration. After that, there wasn't a night when someone in the pine grove wasn't digging with a shovel. The pine grove eventually died out after a few decades of this. There was nothing left of the place by my grandmother's time except a few small trees, wind-swept grass, and Dem Bones on certain nights.

Captain Kidd's skeleton crew is known as Dem Bones. According to my grandmother, they appear in a ship made of shadows. In the dead of night, the ship makes its way up the coast, anchoring near Sandy Hook's shores. Two or three vessels are lowered from her side, each brimming with glowing skeletons in cocked hats and tattered buccaneer garb. Belts laden with handguns and long cutlasses adorn their waists. A skeletal parrot perches on one of the crewmember's shoulders, indicating that he is probably the first mate.

Dem Bones drags heavy vessels brimming with treasure onto the beach and scatters them across the area that used to be the pine grove. One of the skeletons also has kegs and kegs of whiskey, as well as a fiddle, which the pirates take. Dem Bones starts raucous singing and dancing that would reawaken the dead if they weren't already stirring. When the glowing skeletons have had their fill of dancing, they fall on the sand and begin sharing tales of the ships they've seized and the treasure they've amassed.

Dem Bones adorn themselves with gems and pearl ropes as they open the huge trunks. Others throw gold coins around like a child's ball. Dem Bones fill the trunks and row back to the ship of shadows in the deepest hours of the night, long before sunrise. As the glowing skeletons vanish one by one into the hold, the ship draws anchor and sets sail.

15

THE LADY OF THE SMART RING

The night before Christmas in 1798, a wealthy man's wife fell gravely ill, causing him to summon a physician. His wife had apparently passed away by the time the doctor came. Her husband was so upset that he locked himself in his bedroom the next day and didn't turn up for the funeral. The wealthy woman's body was taken to the Vicar, who performed the service swiftly, but poorly due to his inebriation. The iron grille was closed, the stone lid lowered, and the curtain drawn over her forehead.

Before falling asleep later that night, the clergyman recalled the exquisite malachite ring on the thumb of the lady he'd put to rest. He moved downstairs, unlatched the lid, unlocked it, and attempted to pry the ring off, hoping that no one would care. It refused to budge. He dashed away and returned with a file to remove her ring. When that didn't work, he cut off her finger and took the ring. He bent over to pick up the iron grille. As he moved forward to replace it, he cried at the top of his lungs and fled, dropping the bell. With a sinister grin on her lips, the woman rose, cried, and held her dismembered finger.

The woman walked back to her house in nothing but her fine silk robe, banged on the door, and pulled the bell, but no one replied. It was late on Christmas Eve, but all of the servants had gone to bed. She raised a large stone, hurled it at her husband's window, and stood there waiting. With a sorrowful smile on his lips, he came to the window.

To her dismay, he abruptly exclaimed, "Go away! Why do I have to put up with you like this? Aren't you aware that my wife died recently? Allow me to grieve and trouble me no more."

He closed the window, having no idea that the rock had been hurled at the window by his wife. She repeated her action, slamming a rock against the glass once more.

"I am no one but your so-called dead wife," she screamed as he opened the window again. "Unless you want me to die a second time on our doorstep, please come downstairs and open this door."

He asked her, "So you're a ghost, then?"

"No, ghosts don't bleed," she said. "Come down here now before I die of a cold."

16

THE SCROLL OF PIGGY

After a long period of fighting, a married couple decided to seek a divorce. However, when the wife found out she was expecting, they decided to try again, for the child's sake.

After the baby was born, the family enjoyed a brief respite. Sadly, the old issues reappeared soon after, and the father and mother constantly bickered.

When the boy was around five years old, the couple put him to bed, and then they had a huge fight. Enraged, the father wrapped his arms around his wife's neck and choked her to death.

He eventually panicked, realizing what he'd done. If he didn't want to be caught, he had to get rid of the body.

The husband put the body into the trunk of his vehicle and went to a marsh outside of town. He managed to get the body out of the car, but rigor mortis had set in, making transport impossible. His wife's corpse was slung over his back piggyback-style as he paddled out into the foul-smelling marsh. Taking a step backwards, he stood there watching as her rigid hands and miserable face vanished into the gloomy swamp.

The man came home and showered, but he couldn't get the swamp's revolting odor out of his mind. The smell was making him sick to his stomach. No matter how much he scoured or how much he scrubbed, he couldn't get rid of the stink. Wherever he went, it followed him.

The boy became increasingly concerned for his mother as the days passed, and he began asking a lot of questions. His father told him that his mother had gone to live with relatives.

The odor didn't go away. The man tried to ignore it as much as possible. One day, he noticed his son staring at him strangely. When he reached out to his son, the boy recoiled in fear and refused his touch.

On another day, when his son played on the floor, he stepped into the boy's room.

"Son, it looks like something's bothering you. Is there anything you want to tell me?" "Yes, Father."

"Does it have something to do with your mother?" the father asked.

"Yes."

"What exactly is it?"

"Why's Mommy so pale?"

"Could you tell me what you're talking about?"

"Why do you always give her a piggyback ride?"

UNDERNEATH THE BED IS A KILLER

A teenage girl's parents are planning a night out. Despite her youth, she considers herself to be too old for a babysitter. Even though her parents will be out until later, she asks to be allowed to stay home alone. She agrees to call her parents at her usual bedtime so they won't wake her when they get home. In the morning, she will see them.

She's almost asleep when she heard dripping noises. She gets out of bed to see if it's raining outside, but the sky is clear, and the stars and moon are brilliant. She climbs back into bed, shuts her eyes, and hears the dripping echo once more. Her hand dangles from the edge of the bed, and she finds solace in the sensation of a wet tongue licking it. It makes her feel better to know the dog is sleeping under her bed.

She eventually decides she must figure out what the dripping noise is.

The young lady rises from her seat and switches the light on. She continues searching for the source of the noise. The girl checks the hallway, but finds nothing except the photos her family had taken over the years. When she looks in the adjacent bathroom, she can't find anything. Looking within the sink, the faucet isn't dripping. As she examines the shower, not a drop falls from the shower head. The bathtub is completely dry too. Even the toilet has no leaks or anything to explain the noise she's hearing. Finally, when she returns to her room, she goes into her closet to see what she can find. Her dog is dripping blood and hangs with a note that reads, "Humans lick, too."

Printed in Great Britain
by Amazon